Other books by the same author

The Topsy-Turvies
Café at the Edge of the Moon

For Joshua's lovely teachers –
Lisa Gillitt, Linda Nolan, Joanne Hanley,
Norma Freeman, Margaret O'Neill, Nicola Hadley
and the children of Yerbury School
F.S.

For my friends
Max and Nicola Rabkin
P.C.

First published in Great Britain in 1996
Published in paperback in 1997
by Orion Children's Books
a division of the Orion Publishing Group Ltd
Orion House
5 Upper St Martin's Lane
London WC2H 9EA

© Francesca Simon 1996
Illustrations copyright © Peta Coplans 1996

The right of Francesca Simon and Peta Coplans
to be identified as the author and illustrator of
this work has been asserted.

A catalogue record for this book
is available from the British Library
Printed in Italy
ISBN 1 85881 4332

SPIDER SCHOOL

Francesca Simon
Illustrated by Peta Coplans

Dolphin

Kate sat up in bed. It was the first day of school.

"I don't want to go to a new school," said Kate.
"I don't. I don't. I don't."

Kate felt so cross and crabby that she did something
she had never done before.

She got out of bed on the wrong side.

Kate looked at the clock. Nine o'clock. She was going to be late. Where oh where was Mum?

Mum ran into the room. "Hurry up and get dressed, Kate!" she shouted. "You'll be late for school!"

Kate ran to the wardrobe. Her new school clothes were gone. Her new school shoes were gone. Her new school socks were gone, too.

"Where are my new school clothes, Mum?"

"Gone," said Mum. "You'll have to wear something else."

Kate had to wear a dirty old skirt. Her old socks kept falling down. Her old shoes were too tight and squeezed her toes.

"Come on, Kate!" said Mum. They ran down the street. The street was empty. Kate's feet thudded on the pavement.

Clunk-clunk.

Clunk-clunk.

Clunk-clunk.

Then Kate saw her school. The school was big and dark and ugly. It did not look like a nice school. It looked like a dungeon.

Mum left her at the gate.

"Go to Class 3," she said.

"But where is Class 3?" asked Kate.

"You're a big girl. You'll find it," said Mum.

Kate wandered up the hall. Kate wandered down the hall. She found Class 1, Class 2, Class 4, Class 5, Class 6, and Class 7, but not Class 3.

The other children hurried past her. Everyone knew where they were going. But not Kate.

At last she found Class 3. The door was very big.

Kate knocked.
No one came.
Kate knocked again,
a little harder.
Still no one came.

Kate knocked on the door as hard as she could.

The door opened.
It was a gorilla.
"You're late,"
said the gorilla.
"But where is my teacher?" said Kate.

"I'm your teacher, stupid," said the gorilla.

All the children stared at Kate as she tiptoed into
the classroom. She looked everywhere for her
friend Robbie, but he wasn't there.

Kate looked round the room. The
children were sitting on the floor.

There were no tables.

There were no chairs.

There were no pencils.

There were no worksheets.

There were no trays.

There were no posters.

"Where are the
books?" asked Kate.

"No books here," snapped the gorilla.
The children sat still. No one said a word.
The gorilla sat at her desk and read a comic.

Something is not right, thought Kate.

She raised her hand.

"Yes?" said the gorilla.

"Where are the toilets?" asked Kate.

"No toilets at this school," said the gorilla.

The clock ticked loudly. The children sat.

The gorilla read her comic.

Kate raised her hand.

"Yes?" said the gorilla.

"What are we going to learn today?" asked Kate.

"You want to learn?" said the gorilla. "Okay. What's the first letter of the alphabet?"

"A," said Kate.

"Wrong," said the gorilla. "The first letter of the alphabet is Z. Now be quiet. I'm busy."

Something is very wrong, thought Kate.

The clock struck twelve. Dinner time. The dinner lady stood behind a big pot.

Inside the pot were snakes and snails and spiders.

"Excuse me," said Kate.

"Yes?" snarled the gorilla.

"I don't like snakes and snails and spiders," said Kate.

"Oh yes you do," said the gorilla.

"Oh no I don't," said Kate.

"We don't like snakes and snails and spiders," shouted the children.

"Oh yes you do," shouted the gorilla.

"Oh no we don't," shouted the children.

"I won't eat them," said Kate.

"We won't eat them," shouted the children.

"But these spiders are delicious," said the dinner lady.
"And so good for you. Try one with tomato sauce."
And she popped a spider into her mouth.

"Delicious," said the dinner lady. "Try one, Kate,"
And she dangled a big black spider in front of her.

Kate screamed. "I don't want a spider! I don't
want to be at this horrible spider school!
I WANT TO GO HOME!"

Kate ran home as fast as she could. She ran to her
bedroom, took off her clothes, put on her pyjamas, jumped
into bed, pulled the duvet over her head and closed her eyes.

Then Kate sat up, took a deep breath, and got out of bed.

But this time she got out on the right side.

The sun was shining. Mum peeped in at the door.

"Am I late for school?"asked Kate.

"No," said Mum. "It's only seven o'clock."

Kate felt very happy.

Kate put on her new school clothes, ate breakfast, and walked to school with Mum.

Kate's teacher met them at the door. "Hello, Kate, welcome to our school," said her teacher. "I'm Mrs Gillitt."

Class 3 was lovely and bright. There were tables and chairs. There were pencils and worksheets and a tray for Kate. And there was her friend Robbie, reading in the book corner.

"Here's the cloakroom, where we hang our coats and hats," said Mrs Gillitt. "And here are the toilets."

And the school dinner?
Kate had peas, carrots, chips and chicken.
No snakes, no snails, no spiders.

Well, hardly any.